ONE UNIQUE PIECE

Written By

Emily-Anne Willey

Illustrated By

Carla Vidal

Outskirts Press, Inc.
http://www.outskirtspress.com

Paperback ISBN: 978-1-9772-0865-1
Hardback ISBN: 978-1-9772-0977-1

Illustrations by Carla Vidal.

JUVENILE FICTION / Social Issues / Special Needs

Outskirts Press and the "OP" logo are trademarks belonging to Outskirts Press, Inc.

PRINTED IN THE UNITED STATES OF AMERICA

This book is for my Eternal Sunshine, Carla Vidal. Thank you for being you, and proving to everyone you really can be what you want to be when you grow up.

I also dedicate this book to my parents, my husband, Rachel Hollis, and the Alison Show for lighting the fire inside me to Freaking Do IT!

Finally, a huge shout out to every "forever 5th grader" that touched my life and made me the girl I am today.

Her name? Well, she knew her name!
Her name was Carla.

Carla Vidal

She was 10 years old and her family was from Venezuela.
She liked little blue hedgehogs, anything Japanese, and she remembers
everything about this brand-new school she sat in being built, and named,
several months before.
Now, though, in this moment, no one knew any of these facts about Carla.

Miss Johnson was her new 5th grade teacher and had just asked every student to stand up and share a little about themselves.

Carla WAS focused and heard the question. The only problem was that while she formulated her response, she had become distracted by all of the fun things she was learning about her new classmates.

Her teacher asked her again to stand, say her name, and share an interesting fact with the class.

In that moment Carla shot up out of her desk shouting,
"I am Carla Vidal. I have autism."

Miss Johnson didn't know what to do or say. It was her first time teaching, and she had never been trained how to teach with an autistic student in her classroom. She now had an entire classroom full of eyes staring, and waiting to see how she would respond. Calmly, she looked at Carla and said, "That's great Carla. Can you tell us more about autism?"

Carla calmly responded, "Sometimes I act a little strange, and I tend to be emotional, but that's what makes me unique."

All the students looked at Miss Johnson, waiting for her response. Without another moment's thought, she asked, "What else makes you special?"

Carla proceeded to tell the class that she liked to draw,
and she's smart in a lot of ways.

That night, and all throughout the school year,
Miss Johnson learned as much as she could about autism.

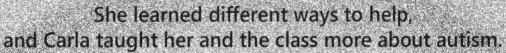

She learned different ways to help,
and Carla taught her and the class more about autism.

Carla taught that autism is much like frosting on a cake. Each cake may be the same, but the frosting is what makes it unique and special. No two cakes are the same. Just like frosting on a cake, autism isn't the same from person to person.

Each day of school was an opportunity to learn how to care for others, recognize their differences, and appreciate how those differences made each student unique.

One Tuesday morning Carla came to school complaining that she did not like having to wear a school uniform, and even worse it had to be tucked in! Her disdain for the uniform had caused her to become extremely emotional right as the school day had begun. She came storming into the classroom screaming and yelling,

The entire class was filing into the classroom and Miss Johnson had to do something. Every student looked with wide eyes at her wondering what to do, and Carla was not able to explain that this meltdown was part of her autism. Miss Johnson looked at Carla and quietly said, "Follow me."

Carla followed Miss Johnson into the hall. This time though, she seemed to be yelling at Miss Johnson about the uniform, as if she could change the rules. Miss Johnson made eye contact with Carla, "Count to 10, and let's talk about this." Carla began to loudly count, "1....2....".

Miss Johnson reminded her that she couldn't yell. Carla spoke in a quieter tone, "3....4....5....6....7". Miss Johnson continued to prompt her to breathe. "8....9....10." Carla said in a normal tone. By the time she had reached 10, she was ready to talk. Carla explained that she was not happy about the uniform and it had caused her to lose control.

Carla came back into the classroom and apologized to the class, explaining that sometimes she gets upset and loses control.

Outside at recess later that day she told a friend that she regretted getting upset, and she was glad that she still had her friends.

There were many days when students would see Miss Johnson and Carla standing in the hall, staring at each other and counting. Sometimes they had to count several times.
It was in those moments that Miss Johnson recognized that Carla was special, just like she had said, and that is what made her unique.

One day Miss Johnson noticed that Carla wasn't paying attention to the lesson. It wasn't that she was distracting anyone, she just wasn't participating in the class activity. Once the lesson was over Miss Johnson invited the class to line up to go to recess.

Carla loved recess, but in this moment she was not listening to anyone around her. Several students tried getting her attention, but it wasn't working. Miss Johnson said in a quiet tone,
"Carla. We are going to recess. What's distracting you?"

Carla shook her head, as if to break herself from her thoughts, stood up and shouted, "Look! The world's longest nose hair!" Carla stood at her desk triumphantly with an imaginary nose hair clutched in her hand.

In that moment, every single pair of eyes quickly darted to Miss Johnson. This was it! How was she going to respond? Miss Johnson looked around the room and into the eyes of the onlookers. These children who had looked to her dozens of times in the past, wondering, waiting, and learning were

wondering what to do next. Those eyes were the eyes of children who had now learned love, compassion, and understanding of those around them. Those same eyes had learned that we are all unique. They were now waiting to see how Miss Johnson would respond. What was she supposed to do?

Finally, she turned away from those watching eyes, looked straight at Carla and said, "ARE YOU SERIOUS!?! The longest?"

The class erupted into laughter.
Each student laughed hysterically along with the two of them.

It was right then that Miss Johnson realized that she had done the right thing. She had taught her class to respect and appreciate each other's differences.

We all do silly things.
We all have crazy imaginations.

We all get distracted. We are all unique.

The author, Emily-Anne Willey is a writer, mom, educator, and traveler. She enjoys writing stories about her experiences of 10 years in public school education. In her free time Emily-Anne loves spending time with her husband and son outside. They enjoy traveling around the world, but Disneyland is their current favorite destination.

Emily-Anne created this book out of a passion for creating awareness and understanding of the students in her classroom, and school. She loved working with Carla during her 5th grade experience, and spreading awareness of autism. Something truly amazing happened that year as students from varying backgrounds came together to truly love and understand one another. Emily-Anne won't say she has a "favorite" class, but it is evident that in this first book of hers she focused on a very special group of kids. This book has been a dream of hers for years. Emily-Anne knew that this book had to be written, and after learning of Carla's skills and college education in illustration it was only natural that the 2 would create something so powerful together.

Emily-Anne would like to thank Carla Vidal for letting her be a piece of her life, both in 5th grade and now. She is so proud of the woman she has become and the fabulous illustrator she is. Your skills and passion are admirable and the world needs you to share your work, and mind. You truly are ONE UNIQUE PIECE.

ABOUT

The Illustrator, Carla Vidal, was born in Salt Lake City in 1995, but it wouldn't be until 2 years later that she would be diagnosed with Asperger's Syndrome, a form of Autism with less than 200,000 cases per year that gives patients developmental disorders involving socialization and communication. Up until 5th Grade, Carla would spend her school years learning under special programs in public schools, sometimes even helping with school-provided lunches if needed. She then transferred to the charter school Navigator Pointe Academy, when she would be learning alongside mainly neurotypical children. Emily-Anne Willey (Miss Johnson), would be the catalyst for Carla breaking out of her shell and making some lifelong friends.

As Carla continued her education in charter school (Paradigm High School), she would discover that her best skills lie in art, where she then took up Graphic Design in Salt Lake Community College, where she graduated in 2016. It would not be a while for her to get a major project until 2017, where Emily came up to her to illustrate this book about her 5th grade experiences.

If I have not told Emily that I was autistic, I would not have been so resilient in keeping my life-long goal of being engaged to the arts. And where I continue from here, I would add another unique piece to the puzzle.

CPSIA information can be obtained
at www.ICGtesting.com
Printed in the USA
BVHW021158040419
544606BV00004B/14/P